D1473964

COFFEE BREAK STORIES

Quick Reads for the Busy Life

by Patricia Carroll-Smith

COFFEE BREAK STORIES

By Patricia Carroll-Smith

© July 19, 2016 by Patricia E. Smith

(Pseudonym – Patricia Carroll-Smith)

To fellow members WHS Class of '54

Happy 80th Birthday!!

TABLE OF CONTENTS

The Side of the Road

A Trip for Morris

At the Mall

The Neighbors

What's Good for the Goose...

Their Way

Fellow

Over Coffee

A Clearer View (Poem)

A stranger and what draws her to...

THE SIDE OF THE ROAD

The day I first became aware of her, I was planting spring flowers in the beds on either side of the front door. It was the prescription issued by the doctor following Byron's sudden death and my lingering depression.

"Get out into the yard. Dig in the dirt. Get your hands dirty," he said.

That day, my back was to the road as I knelt there immersed in the task at hand so I wouldn't have noticed her passing by had it not been for the scuffing sound. The town had not yet cleared away the deposits of sand strewn by the highway department during the winter, and it was this accumulation in which she walked that alerted me to her presence.

Seldom does anyone walk by as there are no sidewalks, so curiosity caused me to sit back on my haunches and pivot toward the sound. I fully expected to see someone I recognized - a neighbor, perhaps - but nothing about her was familiar. Head down, she was advancing slowly. She wore a heavy quilted jacket, woolen tam and gloves though the day was approaching a pleasant sixty-five degrees. From a distance, I judged her age to be close to that of the temperature.

She was nearly past our property when she stopped suddenly at the far side of the driveway. Looking up, she reached both hands into the lilac bush and buried her face deep into the blossoms. The pose made me thing of a lover bestowing a prolonged and passionate kiss. I waited. When she finally drew back, I could see that her eyes were closed, a faint smile softening her weathered features. It was as though the bush had lured her close, then held her captive. An act of subtle seduction. I, too, felt myself transfixed; a voyeur, intruding where I didn't belong. This woman, whoever she was, deserved to be afforded a measure of privacy. Yet, in spite of my misgivings, I found myself calling out to her.

"Hello, there," I said. "Lovely, aren't they?"

Whether she didn't hear me or simply chose not to respond, I wasn't sure. She was still standing facing the bush, hands now clasped in front of her. I made no further attempt to engage her. After some considerable time, she turned, dropped her gaze downward and continued on without a backward glance.

I rose, brushing moist soil from the knees of my jeans and strolled across the lawn and down to the end of the drive. The woman was disappearing around the bend where the road crosses the brook. I watched until she was out of sight then turned and confronted the lilac bush. It had reached its peak, no question. The blossoms were profuse and the aroma intoxicating. It was easy to understand their seductive qualities. I decided to take an armful into the house, carefully selecting blooms from the side away from the road.

Indoors, I searched through the cabinets for the perfect container. Deciding at last on a large, milk-glass pitcher, I arranged the display and carried it to the foyer, placing it on the table beneath the gilt-edged mirror.

The next afternoon I set out to finish my plantings. I went about my work mechanically. I couldn't help thinking about the woman of the previous day, wondering who she was and where she had come from.

I was tamping down the soil around the last of the petunias when my ears alerted me to the sound I had been listening for. That same scuffing, the residue of sand once more announcing her approach. I turned. She was wearing the same jacket and tam. Only the gloves had been shed. Her stance was more erect, her gaze straight ahead. She seemed unaware of my presence.

As I knew she would, she reached the lilac bush and stopped. The scene of the day before repeated itself. This was indeed a love affair, and it caused me to wonder if she had ever displayed the same adoration for any man. I couldn't decide if she was a lonely, tragic figure or one of the fortunate few who recognize and treasure life's everyday gifts. Was she to be pitied or envied?

On day three, I resolved to learn what I could of my mystery woman. I lay in wait, not sure if I would be afforded the opportunity. She did not disappoint. I gave her her moment of privacy, then approached. Trying not to startle her, I called out a greeting as I crossed the driveway.

"Hello," I said. "I noticed you admiring the lilacs."

Again, I was unsure whether she had heard me as she did not turn in my direction. When I reached her side, she spoke, her voice low and husky.

"They're my favorite, don't you know," she said, still facing the bush.

"I'm so glad you enjoy them," I told her. "I thought

perhaps you might like to take some along with you," I said, exposing the clippers in my hand.

"Oh mercy no," she exclaimed. "They're right where they belong."

I felt chastened and repentant. The bouquet in my foyer floated into my mind. I tried another approach. "It's a lovely day to be out walking. Are you visiting nearby?" I asked.

"A rare day indeed," she agreed. "Bright and sunny. That's what they like, you know. Lots of sun. And a sweet soil, lime. Lime spring and fall."

I was getting a lesson in growing lilacs but nothing further. "Would you like to see the rest of the yard?" I asked on impulse.

I wasn't sure if I liked this woman or not, but I was intrigued by her. Was she someone's wandering mother? Eccentric maiden aunt? Respected school teacher? She seemed about to reject my offer so I said, "Please, I'd like to know more about the care of the bush...and my other plants," I added. I could have told her, but didn't, that my husband had done all the yard work, and, in truth, I knew little of what now fell to me.

"How kind, don't mind if I do," she said finally. Hands shoved deep in the pockets of her jacket, she trudged along beside me.

"I'm Cara Hudson," I said, holding out my hand.

"Pleased," she said simply, her hands remaining

where they were.

I ignored the slight, if that was what it was - somehow I didn't think it was intended - and launched into a discourse on the only subject I thought would be of interest to her.

"We've lived here for close to ten years," I told her, still using the *we* out of habit, "and didn't know the first thing about gardening when we moved in. I'm afraid I don't know a whole lot more now," I added, "although I do try."

She made only a little grunting sound in response as I led her around the side of the house. Here, she removed her hands from her pockets and gestured to the vines growing up the side of the chimney. "Those need trimming," she said.

Looking in the other direction, she eyed the bed of iris, one of my personal favorites. I was proud of their size and abundance and anticipated a compliment. "Too crowded," she pronounced. "Need thinning."

Deflated, I slowed, suddenly reluctant to show off the rest of my efforts, but she marched ahead now fully absorbed. I squared my shoulders and trailed along. She was doling out just what I had suggested I was looking for, advice. Why was I now resenting what I saw as criticism?

"You're very knowledgeable," I remarked. "Have you studied botany?"

She looked at me. "No need. Common sense is

all."

When I saw her spy an accumulation of unraked leaves among the ground phlox, I morphed into a school girl, explaining. "It's very hard to rake through the phlox without uprooting the plants."

"They're being smothered, can't breathe," she said, having none of my lame excuses.

The rest of the tour went somewhat better. She admired the flowering dogwood, prescribed tea leaves for the roses and suggested I plant impatiens in a particularly shady area.

When she had seen all there was to see, she turned to go, hesitated, and said, "I thank you for your kindness."

"I appreciate your suggestions," I told her, thinking how childish of me to have been offended. "Feel free to drop in anytime," I added. I knew she never would.

I walked her back to the side of the road. "Do be careful," I cautioned. "Drivers are not expecting anyone to be walking along here." She acknowledged my warning with a slight nod and was on her way.

After that, I continued to gravitate to the front yard each afternoon, using any excuse to observe her. The flowers were in the ground so I turned my attention to digging dandelions out of the expansive lawn. It was necessary work I told myself, unable to admit the real reason for my being there.

She continued to repeat her routine, never returning my wave, never glancing further into the yard. It was as though we had never spoken. Then came the day I noticed the lilacs were beginning to fade. Soon there would be nothing but a very ordinary green bush that would attract no attention until spring rolled around again. I suddenly felt uncommonly bereft.

I waited that afternoon, well past the hour when she was expected. I extracted a dandelion; I glanced toward the road; I extracted another dandelion; I listened. One hour, then two. And then, a sound further up the road. The sand. Not the scuffing but something else. I realized what I was hearing before it came into view. The street sweeper, advancing ever so slowly. I turned and hurried into the house shutting doors and windows against the onslaught.

I stood at the last window watching the big machine pass. It was hugging the side of the road, its whirring brushes stirring up great clouds of dust and dirt. As it passed the driveway, the debris it gathered hovered in the air, forming a veil which descended over the lilac bush like a shroud. I continued to watch it lumber along until it disappeared around the bend where the road crosses the brook.

~~~~~~~~~~~~~~~~~~~

A widow makes plans to full-fill
a promise to her late husband in...

A TRIP FOR MORRIS

*Older lady, plus companion, desires
driver for trip of some length. Must
by of good character with
unblemished driving record.*

Edwina Steinway decided to place her ad under "Personals." There seemed no other way to accomplish her objective. She glanced up to the mantel where Morris resided in a beautiful bronze urn.

"I promised you we'd get there," she told the urn, "and this is the only way."

She re-read what she had written, adding her phone number. "There, that should do it." Heaving a big sigh, she sent if off.

Her next task was to invite her dear friend, Cora Davenport, to sit in on any interviews she lined up as Cora had graciously consented to accompany her on the anticipated trip. As a retired psychologist, Cora would be a good judge of character.

The response to the ad was almost immediate; three replies indicated interest.   Edwina believed a face-to-face interview was the only way to properly assess one's appropriateness for such an important undertaking; thusly, she arranged appointments with each of the prospects on three succeeding days. She would question each very carefully indeed. After all, she was placing her very life and that of her friend's in jeopardy if she made the wrong selection.

Her first choice of candidates, judging by his

distinguished sounding telephone voice, was a Mr. Lawrence Brimley, who arrived promptly at the appointed hour. Mr. Brimley, a gentleman of approximately seventy years, turned out to be as distinguished looking as she had envisioned. Neat in appearance and well-spoken, he stated he was retired and available at a moment's notice.

Edwina ushered him into the living room indicating a seat at the end of the sofa and introduced him to her friend, Cora, already seated at the far end. Edwina settled herself into an easy chair facing them. Minutes later, she had determined that Mr. Brimley was a recent widow and missing his wife of forty years. "Such a fun-loving woman she was," he had told them.

Learning the proposed trip concerned a promise given to Edwina's late husband, "Call me Larry" stated he felt fate had somehow brought them together. Perhaps it had, perhaps it had, thought Edwina.

Not being accustomed to conducting interviews, she suggested they have some refreshments while she decided what pertinent information she needed to pursue. She excused herself, giving Cora the eye to use her skills as she thought best.

Returning with a tray laden with macaroons and lemonade, she noted Mr. Brimley - she did not favor first name familiarity on first meeting - had repositioned himself down next to Cora. Had he just removed a hand from her friend's knee?

Lemonade and goodies gone, Edwina was about to resume the interview when she glanced at Cora who made a covert slashing movement across her throat while she mouthed the word NO. Edwina had never seen her scowl so.

Message received, Edwina rose and thanked Mr. Brimley for coming. "As I think I mentioned" - she wasn't sure she had - "we have other interviews scheduled before we make a determination so we will let you know as soon as we finish. Thank you for coming." She held out her hand.

Mr. Brimley looked reluctant to rise but did so. "Then I'm looking forward to hearing from you," he said. "I know you lovely ladies would be perfectly enjoyable to spend time with," he added, glancing back at Cora who remained seated.

As soon as the door closed behind him, Edwina turned to Cora. "What was that all about?" she asked. "Things looked kind of cozy when I came back."

"That man is a wolf on the prowl," Cora fumed. "The minute you were out of the room he went into his act. It didn't take years of training to access what he was after. And did you hear his remark about how fun loving his wife was?"

"And I was so impressed when I saw him. Cora, dear, do you see now why I wanted you here? Maybe tomorrow will go better," she sighed.

The next day brought a Mr. Frank Corwin to the door. Mr. Corwin was a man of about forty-five to fifty, slightly pock-marked, wearing a jacket that had probably never seen a trip to the dry cleaners. As

Edwina stepped back to allow him to enter, she thought she caught a whiff of something that smelled decidedly like whiskey. Perhaps she was mistaken. She hoped so.

"So, Mr. Corwin," Edwina began when they were all seated, "tell me how you have the time to take an extended trip. Are you unemployed?"

"Oh no, Maam. I got a job, but I can call in sick for a few days. They aint gonna know I aint sick. I done it before."

"I see; but isn't that a little bit dishonest?" Edwina was already getting an uneasy feeling.

"Nah, they gypped me out of overtime last month. They deserve to get screwed."

"I see," Edwina said yet again. She needed a little help here. "Miss Davenport," she said, turning to her friend. "Perhaps you would like to ask Mr. Corwin a few questions."

"Indeed I would," Cora replied, leaning forward. "Mr. Corwin, tell us about your driving record. Is it unblemished as the ad indicated?"

"If you mean did I ever get convicted of any driving offenses, the answer is no. I got one of them radar detection devices, worth the cost."

"And if you hadn't had 'one of them radar detection devices'?"

He smiled. "Well I got one; that's what counts.

And I'd take it along so you wouldn't have to worry."

"I see," Cora responded, echoing Edwina. "I take it you don't hold law enforcers in high esteem."

He gave a non-committal shrug. "Oh they're okay, I guess. You just gotta stay a step ahead of em, ya know?"

Cora glanced at Edwina and indicated she had heard quite enough to render a judgment.

Edwina agreed and said, "Thank you for coming, Mr. Corwin, but I'm afraid you don't meet our qualifications." There was much more she felt like saying, but what was the use. As she closed the door on yet another unsuitable candidate, she groaned.

"I didn't even want to offer refreshments. I don't think lemonade would have been his drink of choice. Oh Cora, what if the last one isn't a fit. No one else has responded to my ad since those three."

Cora put an arm around her. "Have faith; I'll be back tomorrow."

After her friend departed, she approached the mantel. Reaching up, she stroked the side of the urn, a gesture similar to the way she had stroked the side of Morris' head as he lay in the cold, sterile hospital room. Their last conversation had been one-sided, but she knew he was aware of her and everything she'd said. She'd reminded him of all their happy days and years running the music store, omitting their one failure, producing a child, an heir to inherit the thriving business they had built together.

"I'm not giving up, Dear," she told the urn. "I'm overseeing the business; Leonard is doing a good job handling the day-to-day; the books are in fine shape. I can afford a few days away without worrying about the store. I've got one last interview tomorrow, and Lord knows he can't be worse than the last two, but we'll have to wait and see, won't we. He's got a funny name, but I certainly won't hold that against him if he seems acceptable. Otto Carr; that's his name. What do you think of that!"

The appointed time arrived on the following day, and Cora was back taking her usual seat on the sofa. Fifteen minutes later Edwina was wringing her hands and fretting. Ten minutes later still, Cora was figgeting but voicing encouraging words. "He could be having trouble finding his way or having car trouble or any number of things."

"The other two found me okay," Edwina shot back.

"Yes, and promptness was about all they had going for them," Cora reminded her.

"But what if he..." Edwina replied as the doorbell sounded. She hurried out of the room without finishing her thought. When she opened the door, her heart sank. Standing before was a Sylvester Stallone look-alike - Stallone as he looked in his very earliest movies - dressed in jeans and a tee. The tee declared *Life is Short, Live it Up*.

A bit taken aback, all she could think to say was

"You're late!" As an afterthought she added, "You are Otto Carr, I take it?"

"Yeah, non-other," came the reply. "You're Mrs. Steinway?"

"Well, yes I am, but...never mind, you may come in," she said, stepping back. She glanced at the vehicle parked in front as she closed the door. Nothing was ever going to entice her to go anywhere in that! This young man's tardiness was one black mark against him; his jalopy was the second.

"This is Miss Davenport," she said, introducing him to Cora as she indicated a seat on the sofa.

"Hey, that's pretty neat, a piano and a couch!" he proclaimed, to two uncomprehending women. "You know," he clarified, "your names: Steinway and Davenport. Piano and couch, get it?" He chuckled.

Edwina and Cora stared at him. Who or what was this young man who arrived for an interview without the slightest inclination to make a good initial impression.

Cora was first to recover her composure. "Young man, are you aware you are here to be interviewed for a temporary position? Have you indeed ever been on an interview?"

"Oh yeah, sure, plenty of times, but I think a little levity never hurt, do you?"

This was the most relaxed person either of them had ever encountered. It left even Cora, a professional, at a loss. She looked at Edwina with a shrug, which said you might as well get on with it.

Edwina wasn't sure she knew how to deal with someone so utterly unpredictable. "Mr. Carr, Otto," she began. The address Mr. somehow didn't fit. "When you read the advertisement, did you feel qualified as stated?"

"Oh yeah, perfectly. I drive for a living, among other things."

"Really, and what might the other things be, if I might ask?"

"I'm a musician, but gigs don't always come along so I drive for an escort service. And for a funeral home sometimes," he added

"An escort service. I see," said Edwina, glancing at her friend.

"Our company chauffeurs first-time couples around so the ladies feel safe. You can contact them if you want," Otto volunteered. "I'm their No. 1 driver. But it gets kinda tiresome, you know, waiting around outside restaurants and all. But a job's a job."

Edwina sighed. She wasn't sure why she was continuing with this but for the fact he mentioned he was a musician. She wanted to pursue that further for her own satisfaction. "So you say you're a musician. What kind of music do you play? What instruments?"

"I play guitar, mostly country western, but any kind

that'll get me a booking." He took out his phone, searching. "Here we are at our last performance."

He handed the phone to Edwina who saw (could this be the same man?) a guitarist in a beautiful western outfit. With him was a pretty young thing equally garbed.

"That's me and Yummy. We perform together," he explained.

"Yummy?" Edwina said. "That's a stage name, I take it?"

"Oh yeah. Her name's Carolyn Good, but I call her Yummy. Get it? Yummy Good? She likes it so she decided to use it when we're on. She sings and plays."

Edwina declined comment on the name. Her mind was elsewhere. "That guitar," she said, it looks like an older Gibson."

"Yeah, it was my father's. He played with some of the best." He chuckled to himself, remembering. "He was far-out; named me Otto over my mother's objection. Otto Carr. My mother never forgave him, said other kids would make fun of me, but he said he couldn't resist with a name like Carr."

"And did they, make fun of you?" Edwina asked.

"Sure, but they woulda teased me anyway. If it wasn't my name it woulda been my clothes or my crazy relatives or whatever. And Granny said I should just be myself and treat everyone nice no matter what they said or did."

Cora could see that Edwina had gotten off the track, not surprising since Edwina and Morris' lives were totally immersed in the music field. Perhaps she could refocus her friend. "Do you think Mr. Carr, Otto, would like some of your macaroons?" she suggested.

Edwina handed back the phone and jumped up. "Oh, of course he would," she proclaimed, hurrying out of the room.

Cora saw her chance to use her interview skills. This young man would not distract her. "Mr. Carr - better to strike a professional tone - your life seems a bit disjointed. Didn't you ever try to steer it in a more stable direction?"

"Oh sure," he said, "but let me tell you what happened. You see, I had my palm read once, ya know? Anyways, it cost me $15 bucks and, you see this line right here?"

He reached down toward Cora holding out his hand. He traced the line with his fore finger. "She told me this line here was my road to fame and fortune. See it right here? Well, maybe a week later, I picked a knife by the wrong end..." He made a slashing sound. "Now, you see this here scar? It cuts off access to my road to fame and fortune like a big barricade, and now you can't get there from here." He maintained a serious face.

"You don't have a serious bone in your body, do you?" she remarked.

"Just pulling your leg, Miss Davenport. You need to lighten up." Otto grinned.

Cora, the professional, shrunk back into her seat.

"Well here we are," announced Edwina, entering with a tray and setting out her macaroons and three lemonades. "I'm sorry; lemonade is all I have at the moment," she apologized. "No Coke, no Pepsi."

"Hey, I like lemonade, Otto assured her. My granny used to have it for me. You remind me of her," he told Edwina. She was about your size...and her teeth used to clatter." His gaze was somewhere far, far away.

"My teeth do not clatter," Edwina huffed.

"Nah, not that part. That just came to me, that's all. I mean about her teeth clattering. Anyways, I remember her kitchen smelled so good. She used to bake these big peanut butter cookies, and she pressed lines in them with a fork, kind of crisscross like. Sometimes she'd let me help. She had a big sittin-out porch, and she'd bring out the cookies and lemonade. Sometimes she'd stop to play Parcheesi with me or checkers sometimes."

"Sounds like you had a wonderful childhood," Edwina said.

"Not really. Just two weeks every summer, that's all, but I could almost smell those peanut butter cookies clear into winter."

Edwina reached over and patted the back of his hand as they sat in silence drinking their lemonade. She had a recipe somewhere for peanut butter cookies.

Cora was flummoxed by what had just taken place. A bonding for sure. She waited and thought she might suggest that perhaps they had enough information. Still, it really should be Edwina's call.

Finally, Edwina broke the silence. "We have a nice selection of guitars in our store. Maybe you've heard of it, Steinway Music on Stafford Street."

"I've been by it, always wanted to stop in, but it looks a little out of my class," Otto confessed

"Not out of anyone's class," Edwina assured him. "We make accommodations, and you'd be more welcome to come and look around. You could try out some of our models whether you were in the market or not. In fact, I hope you will. Yes, I truly hope you will," she added. "And you could play something for me."

"I could do that without going in," he said. "I got my Lulubelle out in the car; she goes everywhere with me."

"Oh my, could you? Go out and get her? We'd love that, wouldn't we Cora," Edwina enthused.

It wasn't posed in the form of a question, Cora noted, which was a good thing. She had become just an onlooker in this scenario.

Otto needed no further invitation. He was on his feet and headed for the door, leaving Edwina beaming and Cora dumbfounded. "Edwina, dear," she began when they were alone, "is this young man someone you would consider traveling with? That was the point of this, after all," she pointed out.

"Oh don't be so prissy, Cora. That young man is just someone who's comfortable in his own skin, as they say. I think it's refreshing, and yes, I just might consider traveling with him."

Cora was afraid of this. By some devious means, no, that was wrong, the boy wasn't devious, yet he had worked his way into Edwina's trust. He did seem forthright, she had to admit and yet... "Aren't you letting his musical background take on a bit too much importance?" she suggested. "What is he driving," she asked, not having seen how he arrived.

"That's not important," Edwina shot back. "There's my Lincoln sitting idle most of the time. It could use a good long distance run. After all, my little jaunts downtown and back don't keep it in shape. And if he's a good enough driver to satisfy the funeral home..."

"I think you've made up your mind," Cora sighed.

"If you want to back out, that's fine. I just thought a little company on a long ride would be pleasant, but I'd get along." With or without you was implied.

"I have no intention of abandoning you, but you might wait and see if anyone else answers your ad. Just for comparison's sake," Cora added.

"I know all I need to know. Any boy who

reminisces so fondly about his grandmother is a good person."

Subject closed, Cora could see. She knew Edwina better than any of her other friends. This was clearly a case of maternal awakening. How could she fault her here? She knew the Steinways had hoped over the years for a family, but she feared Edwina was leaving herself open for disappointment. This was better left unsaid, however.

Not being particularly musical herself, Cora felt no need to stick around and listen to the performance. "I have to run along," she told her friend, "but you know I'll go along if that is what you decide. Call me tomorrow."

She made her way to the door just as Otto was bursting in with Lullubelle. "Enjoy," she called back to Edwina and was gone.

Cora didn't hear from Edwina the next day, or the next. Curious, she thought she'd better check. "Is everything all right?" she asked when the phone was finally answered.

"Perfectly," came the reply. "I've been tending to company business. That comes first."

Edwina was going make her ask outright. "And...?" she prompted.

"Oh, if you mean the trip, of course we're going. I loaned Otto the Lincoln so he could check it out and get used to it. He's a very good driver, Cora, and he doesn't have a radar detector. In case you were going to ask," she added.

Hmmm, she's in her defensive mode, Cora decided. "I wasn't going to ask," she shot back. *So she loaned him the car.* Her friend was even more taken by this young man than she had realized. What else wasn't she telling? She'd have to keep a closer check on her.

"Have you told him yet that you want to go to Graceland?"

"I did," she said, "and he was absolutely delighted. He loves Elvis's music. Said he always intended to go some day, and he would be happy to help me satisfy Morris' dream. What's more, he wondered if we maybe could include Nashville. Wouldn't that be grand?"

" Marvy," Cora said. She couldn't understand for the life of her why two people with a successful business couldn't have taken time away to do this before it was too late, but there was no point in bringing it up now. She had been more than a little astonished when Edwina had proposed the idea shortly after the funeral. She realized, however, that people deal with grief in many different ways, and if her friend wanted to cart her husband's ashes half way across the country to fulfill an unrealized wish, who was she to question it.

"When were you thinking of going?" she asked.

"Otto has a gig this weekend, but he's free next week. I thought first thing on Monday, if you can make it."

"As good as any time, I guess," Cora sighed, wondering what they were getting themselves into.

Monday arrived all too soon for Cora, but dutifully, she appeared on Edwina's doorstep at eight o'clock. The Lincoln was already parked in front. She left her suitcase on the sidewalk and rang the doorbell. Otto answered, suitably attired in chinos and a nice blue knit shirt. He grinned at her as he lifted two bags, and stepped aside to allow Edwina step out. She was cradling the urn carefully in both hands.

"Here we go, Dear. We're off," she heard Edwina whisper to Morris' remains. To Cora, she said, "You're in the back with Lulubelle. Otto has fashioned a restraint in front for Morris in case I get tired of holding him."

As she entered the Lincoln, Cora noted Lulubelle was already strapped in safely behind the driver's seat. At least her backseat companion wouldn't be boring her with useless conversation, she reasoned.

Otto, a proper chauffeur, saw the ladies seated then took his place behind the wheel. "Take us to Elvis," he instructed the car.

As they pulled away from the curb, Edwina let out a gasp. "Stop the car, stop the car," she shouted.

Otto looked over at her as he braked to a stop. "You've changed your mind?" he asked.

"No, no of course not, but I've forgotten something," Edwina said. "Back up; I have to go back in."

Dutifully, he repositioned the car close to the curb. Edwina had already unbuckled and flung the door open as they came to a stop. "Stay there; I'll be right back," she called to Cora and Otto. She was at the front door in a flash, and unlocking, she disappeared inside.

Returning, she was clutching nothing but a simple paper bag and wearing a big smile. Cora couldn't imagine what could possibly have been so important.

"That's what you had to go back for?" she asked as her friend again settled herself.

"Yes," came the single reply. But Otto, looked over and grinned. "I believe I smell peanut butter cookies. Could it be?"

~~~~~~~~~~~

Jack begins his day...

AT THE MALL

Jack Boynton is late. The mall has been open for close to an hour and unless he hurries, his favorite bench outside of Cinnabon might be taken. He tries to pick up the pace, but his knees are protesting with every step. They are the reason he is behind schedule. You do not go anywhere if the knees aren't doing their job. He wills them to cooperate with the rest of his body. He thinks of them as part of a team, a crucial part, and he will grant them a timeout only after they have completed their task and not before. He pushes forward, shivering in an old jacket too light for today's weather.

Using the Main Street entrance, he leaves the ruckus of the city's traffic behind and finds himself in familiar surroundings. He knows this place well. To the casual observer, he looks neither left nor right as he proceeds along, yet nothing escapes his scrutiny. Late as he is, he takes time to notice each store front, each window dressing, each minute detail.

It's Monday, and he wonders, as he always does, why the high-priced jewelry store bothers to open at an hour unlikely to produce any customers. Out of the corner of his eye, he can see two clerks within. They are meticulously dressed and stand ramrod straight behind counters of glittering merchandise. Already, they wear looks of boredom. He knows this without making eye contact.

As he passes Body Works, he thinks yeah sure, maybe yours works. Maybe he should stop in sometime and see what they do, or sell in there. At Eye Care, a woman sits before a mirror trying on frames. He imagines if he were to return to this spot an hour later, she would still be there, still seeking the perfect look. He understands pride, but he considers vanity a totally frivolous trait.

He takes note of the bank across the way, a small but busy branch of one of the banking giants. He has never been inside, having no business to conduct with them, nor they with him. He knows the manager by sight though, as a frequenter of Cinnabon, which is just up ahead. He coaxes the remaining steps out of his complaining knees and stops before the wrought-iron bench directly across from the entrance to the popular spot. Thankfully, it is not occupied. He eases himself down, aiming for the middle of the bench in the hope that no one will come along and expect to share the seat.

It is good to be here out of the cold. Likewise, on a sweltering summer day the air conditioning is something to look forward to. His room is never warm enough on a day like this nor cool enough in July, with nothing but a small fan sitting atop the chest-of-drawers.

Settling in, he glances over at the nearest trash container knowing full well it is still a bit early for anyone to have discarded the morning newspaper. It's common practice for those doing so to leave it out on top where it could be retrieved. A thoughtful touch, he thinks. Usually, he is able to claim one by noon.

Once in hand, he will turn first to the business page to check whether the market is up or down. Why he does this he cannot explain even to himself, never having had any stocks and not likely to have any in the future through inheritance or any other means. He knows of no wealthy kin just waiting to surprise him.

The weather forecast will grab his attention next. It will tell him how much longer his joints have to tolerate the current cold snap. This, too, is pointless. His body will have to accept whatever Mother Nature has in mind for the rest of the winter. As for the rest of the paper, each section gets its proper attention in due time. He has all day so why rush.

Sometimes a section will be missing or an article torn out. If he's lucky, the crossword puzzle will be left undone. If worked on, he prides himself on finishing it. It means the gray matter is still functioning pretty well.

This bench he has selected is a prime location. Businessmen and store managers exiting the shop with their large, covered coffee cups are accustomed to seeing him sitting here. He envisions them offering loose change which he just might accept. Soliciting is, of course, forbidden but, more than that, he has his pride to consider, and asking for a handout is a practice he would never stoop to. Rather, he would think of accepting their offerings as relieving them of the annoyance of having the change weighing down pockets already burdened with wallets and car keys.

Timing is everything. By late morning the customers are mostly women shoppers. Women would never offer anything. They generally pass by in pairs and are too busy chatting away to take notice. The ones who do happen to glance his way wear *that* look as they veer slightly closer to the storefronts. He has seen enough of *that* look to last a lifetime. If one were to ever approach, he would flat out refuse her offering. He would draw himself up just as straight as possible and manage, he thinks, to look highly indignant as he proclaims, "Madam, you offend me. I believe you have mistaken my intent as I pause here for a bit of rest." She would then murmur an apology and hurry on her way.

Today is shaping up to be a particularly slow day. The aroma emanating from the shop is getting the best of him. He will have to part with what little he has in his pocket for a coffee and warm, tempting cinnamon roll. Money is especially low since he forked over his monthly rent last week.

He is about to rise and risk losing his seat when a young woman leaves the shop and approaches, looking a bit frazzled.

"Excuse me," she says, addressing him. "This sounds crazy, but could you help me out?"

Help her out? What could he possibly do for her? He can't even help himself out.

Before he can respond, she continues on. "I don't know where my mind is lately. Today was my turn to go out and fetch the 'coffee and'." She holds out a large bag from the shop. "Here it is and would you believe it? I totally forgot that Doris is on vacation, and I ordered for her as well, and I can't go back looking totally foolish. She always wants a coffee light with two sugars so that's what I got. Could you possibly take it and the roll I got for her so I won't have to go back and admit I'm a total dunce? Please?" she concludes separating out the extra order from her purchase.

Well, he supposes he can't very well refuse to help someone out of a predicament. It wouldn't be gentlemanly, would it? "If it would help," he tells her, straightening up. "I will accept."

"Oh, you're a lifesaver," she enthuses, thrusting them into his hands. "Thank you so much." Without giving him an opportunity to respond further, she darts away.

He gazes down at the unexpected windfall and fails to see her smile and wink at a fellow standing just off to the side.

The coffee is sweeter than he is accustomed to but nice and hot. And the roll... What is more heavenly than this! He takes his time, making it last, relishing every bite. What a stroke of luck! He thinks of the girl, a rattle-brained young thing for sure. He hopes she is better at her job than she is at getting a coffee order straight.

As he finishes, he drops the drained coffee cup into the trash container and settles in to watch the passersby and wait for his newspaper. Not a bad start to the day after all.

~~~~~~~~~~

Good-Hearted woman wants to help

THE NEIGHBORS

A car horn blared in the street. Ada knew it wasn't meant for her. No one had sat outside the house tooting for her since goodness knows when. She hurried to the front window suspecting what was going on.

Pulling the curtain aside, she gave a deep sigh. Sure enough, there was Old Pa in the middle of the road, traffic now backing up behind him. Broom in hand, he was sweeping the street. Yet again. He had worked his way down the block and was now directly in front of her house.

She shook her head in slow motion. "That poor soul," she murmured. He'll be hit one of these days, she thought, as she turned away to look for her sweater. Moments later she was hurrying out to intercept him. The effort was considerable; she wasn't so young herself and suffered painful feet from fallen arches. Her excessive weight didn't help matters, yet she moved rather quickly when the occasion demanded.

The horn blower had his window open shouting obscenities. He was a middle-aged man old enough to exhibit some control, and Ada hollered back at him.

"Keep your britches on. Can't you see he's an old man?" She suspected Old Pa was subjected to enough verbal abuse from those no-good grandsons of his without this.

"C'mon now," she said softly as she reached his side and steered him to the sidewalk. She had a firm grip on his arm, and he had little choice but to follow along beside her. When he was safely out of the street, she relaxed her grip, half afraid that she would be responsible for one of his brittle bones snapping in two.

The driver added a crude gesture and some further obscenities as he gunned the engine and took off. The other drivers in line merely gawked at the scene on the sidewalk; a solidly plump apron-clad woman holding on to a stooped, scarecrow-of-a-man grasping a broom. The scene would no doubt be recalled at several dinner tables that evening.

"That's enough for today," Ada told her captive, patting his arm. "Come along inside for some cookies, then I'll walk you home." The bribe never failed.

She led him to the kitchen door and waited patiently while he transferred the broom to his other hand so he could grip the railing and haul himself up the steps. It was a routine he was familiar with, occurring with great regularity of late. She held the door open, taking the broom from him and propping it up against the railing. He offered no protest, giving it over willingly and stepping into the house.

Ada's kitchen was large and bright and spotless. The windows shone and the curtains were crisp with starch. The appliances, though old, but had been waxed to a gleaming luster to compete with the linoleum floor.

She led the old man directly to the sink where she turned on the tap and held out a bar of soap. There would be no milk and cookies without clean hands. She had raised five children, and her rules had not changed. The old man complied, while Ada resisted the temptation to get out a brush and scrub under his nails.

She pulled a chair out and guided him into it. She would serve him a snack and a lecture. He would accept the one and discard the other, no doubt. The lecture might be useless, but the snack was not. She suspected he was malnourished.

She opened the refrigerator and pulled out a quart of milk. Behind it was a container of buttermilk. She extracted the buttermilk, returning the two percent. Buttermilk disgusted her, but she had learned the old man was fond of it so she regularly kept it on hand. She poured a large glassful and set it before him.

Oatmeal cookies were piled under the dome cover of the cake plate on the counter. She reached for a napkin and placed four large cookies on it, replacing the cover. From experience, she knew better than to place the entire batch before him. having done so on a previous occasion. Clearly, he had been hungry, and she didn't begrudge him, but he had seemed bent on making himself sick. After that, she simply doled out what she deemed to be a generous but appropriate helping.

Placing the cookies in front of him, she settled herself heavily into the chair at the opposite end of the table. She willed herself to ignore the strong body odor wafting her way. It fought with, and overpowered, her own gardenia-scented talcum. If he had been a child, she would have marched him to the bathroom, drawn a warm tub and thrown him in. Then she would have gathered up his clothes - all of them - and tossed them out. One of these days, she thought, she just might walk him down to the barber shop and slip Vinnie a few dollars to give him a shave and a haircut.

She watched him down his buttermilk, smacking his lips. He picked up a cookie, broke it and carefully picked out the raisins, placing them on the bare table.

"Raisins are no good," he grumbled, speaking more to himself than to her.

"Those are the only kind I have today," she told him. "Eat up." She rose, retrieved the buttermilk container and refilled his glass.

He quickly finished off the contents together with the cookies. Then he raised his hand and swiped it across his mouth. It was the signal Ada had been patiently waiting for.

"Now listen to me, Henry," she began.

He raised his hand as if to ward her off. "I told you. Don't call me that," he growled. "I'm Old Pa. O L D P A," he emphasized.

Ada knew very well that everyone called him Old Pa, and why. It started at home. His son was Pa to his boys, so he had become Old Pa to his grandsons and eventually to everyone else. Ada had resisted referring to him in what she felt was a disrespectful manner, but every time she tried to use his given name, he would stubbornly correct her. The only reason she could think of was that, in his mind, "Old Pa" kept him connected to family. This would have been vitally important to him, for the story was, that he had lost his parents and both sisters back in the old country during the war. Or perhaps he was simply not comfortable with the

Americanized version of his name.

Sometimes, on his better days, he would give her little glimpses into his past. His father had been a tailor and his mother, a hausfrau. Ada had pieced together over time a story of peace and harmony turned suddenly chaotic and finally, unimaginably tragic. The telling of even a bit of the tale would reduce him to tears, so she never encouraged him. She wasn't sure she could bear to hear more at any rate.

Eventually, he had found his way to this country, married, and raised a son. By all accounts, the son had been in serious trouble from an early age, and Ada knew first-hand that the grandsons were turning out no better. There had been neighborhood thefts and vandalism, and all fingers pointed to the boys.

"Okay," she conceded. By any name, the message was the same. "You must stay out of the street; it's too dangerous. If you must sweep, sweep the sidewalk. Are you listening to me?"

He looked up. "You're a good woman, Missus," he said. His rheumy eyes scanned the room as if seeing it for the first time. "My mother kept a house like this, real clean and tidy like. And she swept the street. She took pride."

His voice trailed off. He was in another time, another place. Almost as an afterthought, he added, "We were happy, very happy."

Ada let him drift awhile, awash in the distant past. She suspected there was little enough pleasure in his days, and dreaded handing him back to that rowdy bunch up the street. Where was the justice?

She rose and reaching across the table, scooped up the discarded raisins and folded them into his napkin, then carried napkin and glass to the sink. It's time to go home," she said, turning.

He was already pushing himself back from the table. Each time she saw him stand, she had the same thought. Were it not for the suspenders, his pants would surely end up around his ankles. The old flannel shirt, though tucked in, did little to fill in the gaping space between the shrunken body and baggy trousers. It made her wish she had not given away her husband's clothes.

She slipped her apron off and replaced her sweater. Then she took the old man's arm and marched him toward the door. For her, the feeling was always the same: the duty-bound guard escorting the prisoner to the gallows. She wondered what went through his mind.

They retrieved the broom and proceeded slowly along. To observers, they might have been a long-wedded couple out for a pleasure stroll; two people comfortable with each other and their station in life. They picked their way, carefully avoiding the humps and cracks in the pavement. The sidewalk was old; the neighborhood was old; the houses were old. But the houses and tiny yards - save the one to which they headed - were well cared for. Window boxes spilled over with geraniums here, petunias there. Front doors displayed seasonal swags or cheerful Welcome signs. Lawn ornaments were plentiful and ranged from cute to tacky.

The old man's property was similar only in size to those on the rest of the street. Ragged shades hung in otherwise bare windows. The house, which had once been yellow - or cream, perhaps - bore the look of abandoned property. An old bedspring rested against the side of the house while Queen Anne's lace grew up and out through the coils. The effect was that of a ludicrous attempt at modern art. Other less decorative weeds sprouted randomly through cracks in the driveway.

At the far end of the driveway, was an old junk of a car with a bumper sticker that threatened "BACK OFF" and another that Ada couldn't make out. Just as well, she thought.

The house, as she understood it, had been Henry's and his wife's. After her death, the son - now with a wife and kids in tow - had returned and cajoled the old man into signing it over. That was some years back. Since then, the daughter-in-law had fled, and the two boys had grown up. They appeared to Ada to be in their late teens or early twenties, unemployed and up to no good.

Today, one, or both, were apparently home as a deafening ruckus permeated the walls of the house as they approached. It was the same pounding beat that she often heard from cars driving by. No wonder the poor man escaped whenever he could!

It was Ada's habit to leave her friend to make his own way up to the back door, but today she just kept walking with him. It hadn't been her plan to confront whoever was home, but there was no time like the present to give someone a piece of her mind.

She marched up and knocked on the door. She waited. Useless, she thought. Her knock was no match for the sound within. Ada was not leaving. She grabbed the broom from the old man and beat on the door with the handle. After a fashion, the door burst open.

Before her stood what she took to be the older of the boys. He was clad in a tank top and jeans. Ada noted his spiked hair and glanced at his bare arms. She expected to see them covered in tattoos, but she saw none. It was the first time she had gotten a close look at him.

She squared her shoulders. "Is your father home?'

"Whataya want him for?" He sounded surly, which she had expected.

"Never mind that. Is he home?"

"Nah, he aint." The boy stood with one arm braced across the doorway as if expecting her to barge into the house.   The old man hung back, unable or unwilling to go in. Further into the room, she could see a girl lingering. A faint, sweet smell drifted out. Ada knew what it was. She had been through a hard time with one of her own sons, but she had dealt swiftly and harshly.

"When will he be back?"

A faint smirk. "When he gets good and ready I guess. How should I know, I ain't his keeper."

Ada persisted. "Well who's supposed to be watching after your grandfather? He'll be hit out there one of these days." She gestured toward the busy street.

"I ain't his keeper, neither."

She was getting nowhere. She had instilled a certain amount of respectful fear in her own sons at that age, but they had been under her roof. That leverage didn't apply here.

"Look, this is your grandfather," she said. "He needs someone watching out for him."
The kid threw up his hands. "Be my guest, lady. You got nothin better to do."

"C'mon, Buzz. I gotta split soon," the girl within whined.

"Yah, I gotta go, lady. Get on in here, Old Pa," he hollered over Ada's shoulder.

The old man moved up as Ada stepped aside. Without a word he stooped and ducked under the boy's arm and disappeared into the house.

"Nosey bitch," she heard as the door slammed in her face.

Ada stood there regaining her composure before making her way back down the drive. All the way home she pondered the situation. She could phone Elder Affairs and ask that someone make a house call. She could take him in herself; she had plenty of room. No, she enjoyed her peace and quiet. If she reported the family, would those boys, or their father, extract revenge? Even so, could she just do nothing? It was time to take action, but what action?

So deep in thought was she that she failed to sidestep the raised crack in the sidewalk in front of her own house. She hit it with the toe of her shoe. Her foot stopped abruptly, but her upper body continued its forward motion. In a flash, she found herself sprawled out, facedown, the wind knocked out of her. She lay there, nose to the pavement.

A vehicle braked beside her. She couldn't turn to see it, but she could feel the heat issuing from it. A door slammed, two doors, then a man's voice.

"Are you okay, ma'am? And a voice on the other side. "We'll call an ambulance."

The indignity of it! "No, don't. I'm all right. Just help me up." She was speaking into the ground, no chance of looking at her rescuers.

"Are you sure, ma'am?" from the voice on her left.

"I'm sure. Help me up." Two strong hands reached under her arms and lifted, helping her to her knees. Her head was reeling. Another hoist, and she was standing. She felt lightheaded, and her knees wanted to buckle. She tried to get her bearings. A pickup, four-ways flashing, idled beside her. Two husky young men kept her supported.

"I wonder if you could help me to the house," she asked.

"You sure you're okay?" asked one.

"Perfectly," she lied. Everything hurt, but a good rest and she'd feel better.

The steps up to the kitchen door were the hardest, but the easier front-door entrance was locked. Once inside, she directed the young men to a chair where they deposited her and then left after her assurance she would call someone to look in on her.

So tired. An hour passed as she dozed. On waking, she wished for nothing more than a cup of nice strong tea, but the effort was more than she could muster. She glanced at the clock. Five fifteen. "Oh my," she said aloud. She reached for the phone and dialed Liz Benson next door. Liz was newly home from the hospital with twins, and Ada had promised to fix dinner and run it over. The beef stew was all made and needed only to be heated. She had planned to make dumplings at the last minute, but that wasn't going to happen. She had stiffened up badly during her snooze and wasn't sure she could rise from the chair.

Liz answered after the fourth ring, and Ada related that she had had a small mishap and could Liz send Doug over for the stew. "No prob," she was assured. Doug was home and he would stay with the babies. She'd be happy to escape for even five minutes.

Her neighbor knocked and came right in. She followed Ada's voice through the kitchen to the sitting room and stopped short. "God, what happened?" Liz was frozen in mid-step, her mouth open.

"Nothing really," came the reply. "Just tripped and fell out there on that sorry excuse for a sidewalk."

Liz came closer. "But look at you, she cried. "Skin off your nose, your eyes turning black, your knees all skun, just for starters.

"I'm fine, really." Ada wasn't used to having anyone fuss over her.

"Yea, sure," said Liz as she reached for the phone. "Doug," she said, can you handle things for a bit? I'll be home in half an hour or so. Call if you have any problems." She hung up and turned to Ada.

"Now," she said, hands on her hips.

A short time later, Ada sported an array of band aids and had a heating pad against her lower back. A cup of steaming tea sat on the end table next to her chair.

Liz was standing over her, holding the pot of stew. "Don't move from that chair," she commanded. "I'll take this home and heat it up and be back after I nurse the twins."

Ada opened her mouth to protest, but Liz was off. "Remember, stay put," she hollered over her shoulder and was gone.

The house was quiet save the sound of traffic outside. That brought her back to the problem of Henry. She felt a need to do something, but what? She couldn't think. Perhaps tomorrow… She dozed off again. When she woke, Liz was again standing over her, touching her arm.

"I've brought you back some of your stew. It was delicious, by the way, she added. "Do you think you can make it to the kitchen if I help?"

Ada thought so, but first, a more pressing problem. With Liz to lean on, she rose slowly and made it to the bathroom while Liz waited at the door to help her to the table.

The warm stew - along with heat-and-serve rolls Liz had supplied - found Ada feeling better. While she ate, she told Liz about walking Old Pa home and her encounter with the grandson.

Liz shook her head. "That bunch is bad news; don't get involved." Easy to say. She knew Ada all too well. "You should have been a missionary," Liz ventured.

"Don't worry about me," Ada said. "You just get yourself home and tend to those darling babies. If I can make it over tomorrow, I'll watch them if you need to run to the store."

Liz laughed. "You need a babysitter yourself right now. I'm doing fine." She leaned in. "Seriously," she said, "don't you think you ought to be checked out? Make sure you're okay?"

"Not on your life," declared Ada. "I'm allergic to doctors."

Liz threw up her hands. "Hokaay, but you know I'm

only a minute away." She rose and cleared the table.

Ada stood and checked her steadiness. "You leave those things and get on home. Scat. Shoo." She flicked her wrist playfully then wished she hadn't. It reminded her to stop at the bathroom medicine cabinet for the Tylenol.

Locking up after Liz's departure, she shuffled around flicking off lights. It would be the first time ever that dirty dishes remained in the sink overnight. She envisioned a long soak in a nice warm tub, but discarded the idea in favor of heading straight to bed.

Turning down the covers and undressing was more of an effort than she realized, but finally she settled down. She experimented with several positions. Laying on her back proved to be the most comfortable. She stared at the ceiling. The fine cracks in the plaster were invisible in the near dark of the room, but she knew they were there. Cracks in the ceiling, cracks in the sidewalk, cracks in imperfect lives, she thought as she drifted off.

Somewhere near morning, REM sleep took over. *Ada was sitting on her front lawn nursing Liz's twins at her ample breasts. Old Pa sat amidst a spreading patch of Queen Anne's lace eating a bowl of stew. Liz poured buttermilk into the cracks in the sidewalk. A pickup floated by in the street. In big, bold letters, a bumper sticker announced LEND A HELPING HAND.*

Ada rolled over, and a ray of light broke through a crack in the bedroom drapes and woke her to the start of a fresh new day and a resolve to find help for Old Pa.

Turnabout is fair play
Isn't it?

WHAT'S GOOD FOR THE GOOSE...

Hello, my name is Phoebe and I'm an introvert. There is no help group for me that I know of, but it's okay; I really don't need one. I've faced my problem, and my friend, Fiona, has volunteered to guide me toward a fuller life.

I met Fiona at a prayer meeting, and she just kind of imposed herself on me, I guess. I must have looked needy. Anyway, Fiona took me under her wing, and I became her project. We started meeting for weekly lunches at one of the popular cafes in the West End. She would select the table and order for both of us.

I considered Fiona to be quite worldly. She was a rather big woman, a bit too amply endowed in a couple of places, but she carried herself with a grace and assurance that I admired. Perhaps it was those qualities, which she seemed to think I lacked, that interested me, and I became a willing student under her tutelage.

I remember the first time we got together. She began my makeover as soon as we were seated. Reaching across the table, she patted my arm (she was always patting my arm) and said, "Phoebe, you know I love you dearly, but you really mustn't slouch." She waved the back of her hand in front of my face indicating I should raise my chin.

I adjusted my posture immediately, and looked over to see her scanning my features with that all-knowing eye of hers. She pronounced my eyebrows poorly shaped and my lipstick too pale for my dark hair and eyes.

"Trust me," she cooed. "Fiona knows best." This, before our lunch had even arrived. I, of course, thanked her and made mental notes for later. I checked out the clam casserole in front of me, which was not particularly appealing, but I needed to impress Fiona with my willingness to go along with her plan for me so I dove in while she again reminded me of my posture.

I think it was at our second get-together over Polynesian something-or-other that I learned that I should be wearing bright reds and yellows instead of my preference for pastels. "So you don't fade into the background," I was told. At this early stage, hiding in the background was the idea, but I deferred to her better judgment. I calculated my budget might allow for one new outfit, and I would be sure to wear it at our next session. I had begun thinking of our lunches as "sessions."

I should note here that my mentor began every "session" with a pat on the arm and "I love you dearly" then I would wait for her "but." There was always a "but" coming, and I would brace myself. What flaw would she divulge this time that I would be grateful to have corrected.

One week, I needed to work on the timbre of my voice. Apparently, I wasn't projecting properly. Another time, I was instructed to closely observe those around me, selecting those qualities that made them stand out in the crowd. This one bothered me as I didn't want to be seen staring; they might stare back.

Next time, she produced a list of reading materials from which I could benefit. I glanced at titles like

"Come On Out of the Shadows," "Polish That Image and Shine" and "Dare to be Daring!" WOW, I thought; my mentor has set high goals for me! I mustn't disappoint.

These suggestions have been going on for as long as I've known Fiona - weeks now - and apparently she has determined I have yet to reach my full potential, but I have a surprise for her. I have advanced far beyond my own expectations. I'm fairly bursting with self-confidence.

Fiona has done an admirable job, but it's time to move on, and I'm ready to return the favor. She has been so good to me that I now feel empowered with a new hair style, a new posture, a new well-modulated voice, a whole new persona. So in appreciation of all this nurturing, I feel it's time to give back and today - this very day - I intend to thank my friend. She will be so pleased that in my newly developed confidence, I can now point out to her something that will improve her overall appearance.

We meet as usual. I'm wearing red, my hair frosted, my eyebrows properly shaped. I 'm already seated in a booth instead of our customary table when I see her enter. I wave my hand to redirect her, and she struts over in that way that I've recently begun to notice.

I watch as she squeezes that wide rear of hers into the seat opposite me. "I've already ordered," I tell her. "For both of us."

She gives me a surprised look, raised eyebrows and all. "Oh?" she says.

"Yes," I tell her. "I thought we'd try something different. She surveys her plate as the waitress sets out a cup of minestrone and a tuna wrap in front of her.

"Hmmm, different," she mutters. She drums her fingers on the table, mulling over a more coherent response; and I notice, for the first time, chipped nail polish.

Before she has time to add anything further - I'm so excited - I reach over and pat her arm and say "You know, Fiona, I love you dearly." Her eyes widen, nostrils flare, senses alert, "but you really need to do something about that BIG BUTT of yours."

Oh dear, I really didn't mean to emphasize it like that. Flustered, I hurry on. "Anyway, I have found just the help you need, an exercise program," I tell her, reaching into my purse for a printed sheet. I'm about to hand it to her when I notice she has turned the most brilliant shade of crimson, not too becoming, by the way, with her hennaed hair.

I have never seen my friend speechless until now. Perhaps she's choking on something which could account for her florid face. Now I'm really alarmed as she attempts to rise, upending her glass of ice water which soaks and ruins her sandwich. When she finally manages to stand, she turns and heads straight for the door without a word or look in my direction.

I'm left holding the sheet of exercises up out of the way as the waitress, who has hurried over, sops up the spill. "I was only trying to help," I say half to myself.

When order has been restored, I finish my lunch. As I'm leaving, I notice a woman sitting alone in a quiet out-of-the-way corner. Her gaze is down and she seems to be trying to disappear from view. In my new awareness, I can spot someone in obvious need. I hurry over and introduce myself.

"Hello, I'm Phoebe," I say, reaching out to give her arm a little pat.

A grandmother needs to let go in...

THEIR WAY

There was a time when Lydia English would have tactfully declined tea served in a foam cup, not that any of her friends would have ever done so. But now she looked up from her place at the end of a sagging sofa into the face of a rather lovely young woman holding out just such an offering. The teabag string and tag dangled over the cup's edge like a markdown ticket announcing its reduced status.

"I remembered," the girl beamed. "Tea, not coffee."

"Thank you, dear," Lydia said, hoping she sounded duly appreciative. In fact, she was indeed appreciative, grateful even to have been invited.

The girl reached down and gave the older woman's arm a little pat. "I'll be right back with a plate," she purred and retreated past other guests and into the kitchen. Heather. That was her name. Lydia had had such a time remembering in the beginning. She had finally observed that it rhymed with feather and had pictured her wearing a headband suitably adorned. A blond, permed Indian maiden. It had taken this odd association to do the trick. She would not forget the girl's name again.

Reaching over the arm of the sofa, she set her cup down on the TV tray which served as an end table. This was her first visit to her grandson's apartment. Or was it Heather's? Two years ago she had vowed never to set foot in this place, but times change, and one can choose to either accept or be brushed away like a fall of dandruff on navy serge. So here she sat, hoping to blend in and wondering if she would ever be able to rise from the sink hole she had settled into.

Her head ached. The pounding beat of the music on the opposite wall threatened to consume her. She tried to shut it out by focusing on Malcolm. Malcolm - God rest his soul - would have approved of her decision to come. Malcolm the peace maker. How many times had she heard him say, "C'mon now, Lydie, life's too short to dwell on the negative." Malcolm the saint. How she missed that man!

Even in death, it was he who had brought the family together again. She recalled a tearful Matthew returning, so anguished by his grandfather's sudden passing that she had had no thought but to rush to comfort this only son of their only daughter. Gone at that moment, though not entirely forgotten, were the disappointments and resentments that had left them all adrift.

She had remembered Matthew then as the toddler who gave his grandfather so much joy, an antidote for the son she had never been able to give him. And she saw him as the adolescent who learned to swim, to use a compass, to play a passable game of chess, all under Malcolm's tutelage while the child's own father distanced himself by signing on for one tour of duty after another.

She had refused, for the sake of Malcolm's memory, to remember him as the rebellious teenager who had fled from them after high school graduation, rejecting their offer to fund his further education. It hadn't been a pretty scene. Words had flown. Ill-considered, hurtful jabs like "thankless" and "ungrateful." from a rejected grandmother. Retorts of "controlling" and "manipulating" from a previously dutiful daughter. And mumbled curses from a floundering young man reaching for independence.

Only Malcolm had backed away to assess the scene sanely. She recalled his words so clearly. "We've been wrong, Lydie - both you and me - we've been wrong. We tried to mold Matt like a piece of clay into some sort of stand-in for the perfect son we both imagined having. We've been wrong," he'd repeated yet again.

Blessedly, he had spared her by not detailing each and every error of their ways, but she had seen him grow quieter, maybe even dispirited. He took Matthew's rejection hard, not to mention the cooling of the relationship between daughter and parents. Lorraine had drawn strength from her son's stand and blossomed on her own. A divorce followed by a move to a more distant city had further accentuated their loss. And now here she was - Lydia English - putting aside her convictions, trying to reconnect.

She studied the other guests, Matthew's and Heather's friends. They were standing in groups of twos and threes chatting amiably. Their beverage of choice, Budweiser. No frosted steins or even foam cups here, just bare naked cans meeting thirsty lips. No one acknowledged her presence. She tried in vain to hear their conversations over the racket from the stereo. But what did it matter anyway; they surely weren't discussing the upcoming season at Tanglewood nor the benefits of vitamin E. Of course they weren't, and why should they? They were aliens from another age speaking a language entirely indecipherable to her.

She reached for her foam cup and took a sip of the weak, lukewarm drink which passed - barely - for tea. Added to the TV tray was a paper plate apparently placed there while she had been absorbed in thoughts of the past. It contained a mound of chili and a couple of pickle spears next to a handful of Fritos. Alien food.

She had made a mistake in coming. Why on earth had they invited her? Matthew seemed to be busy in the kitchen, and except for a quick, awkward hug when she arrived, she had seen no more of him. Did he not realize how out-of-place she would feel? Then again, what had she expected? That he would have invited her friends? Of course not, but she'd had the impression she was to be the sole guest, not that he had said so when he called. She had merely assumed as much.

She longed to be back in her own place, back surrounded by all things familiar. She wanted to nestle down in Malcolm's recliner, the closest thing to feeling his arms around her. The afternoon sun would beam in, warming her. It would mean that she would invariably doze off, but that was all right. It made the time go by. She sometimes dreamt when she dozed there, but never of Malcolm. Why was that when her daydreams were of nothing but their days together? Yes, she could orchestrate her daydreams, but the rest she had absolutely no control over. That was hardest of all.

"Gram, Gram! Are you okay?"

She looked up through unfocused eyes at the figure

first standing and now hunched down in front of her. She forced herself back to the present. Matthew. His two hands rested on her knees, a look of concern on his face. Other faces across the room were turned in their direction. Curiosity? Indifference?

"I've been talking to you, but you didn't seem to hear me," he began. He rose easily, and took a seat beside her. "Sorry, I know you must have felt deserted, but I was trying to help Heather with the chow."

Lydia looked at her grandson, so handsome, so familiar and yet...what was it? Something she couldn't quite put her finger on. In the two years since she had last seen him, he had filled out, put on weight, and it suited him. But there was something more, an air of self-confidence, she decided, which had been sadly lacking in his teens. She couldn't resist checking to see if he was still biting his nails down to the quick. He wasn't.

She opened her mouth to reassure him she hadn't felt deserted. It would have been the proper thing to do, but nothing came out. She reasoned she had spent her entire life letting loved ones off the hook. Take Lorraine and her infernal excuses for forgetting her mother's birthday or neglecting to return phone calls. It was always "Don't worry about it, dear; you have a lot on your mind." Lorraine would greedily accept the absolution, agreeing she was indeed leading a busy life and that would be that. Until the next birthday, or Mother's Day.

Matthew waited, expecting the same vindication. When none was forthcoming, he continued on. Spying the untouched plate of food next to her, his look turned sheepish. "Sorry again. About the food, this time. I didn't think. I'll see if Heather can find you something more suitable."

She waved the suggestion away. "I'm fine; just not hungry," she told him, knowing full well he would not pursue it further. There I go again, she thought, at the same time wishing for a nice finger roll filled with seafood salad and maybe some dainty cookies.

"So how do you like our place?" He gestured with a sweep of his arm.

Our place. His and Heather's. He knew she had disapproved two years ago when they moved in together. Yes, she was old-fashioned, out-of-step with the times. Lorraine had told her as much, but it hadn't changed her mind. She remembered Matthew bringing his new girlfriend to meet her. It was shortly after they had put Malcolm to rest. The girl with the hard to remember name. She seemed pleasant enough, pretty but not too pretty. Soft spoken, a little shy or maybe just uncomfortable meeting her boyfriend's grandmother.

They had stopped by in the early evening, the time of day somehow hardest for her, the time when she and Malcolm would have been sitting enjoying an after-dinner glass of wine or cup of tea. The hardest because the fussing and fiddling that occupied the day and locked out much of the loneliness was done, and the quiet had descended. She had been pleased to see them, offering them tea. She knew it wasn't the right thing to offer, but she kept no soda in the house. They had politely suggested coffee as an acceptable alternative.

And so they had sat in companionable silence sipping their coffee while she finished her cup of tea.

Matthew had taken the lead then informing her that he and Heather had found an apartment on Crescent. Lydia knew vaguely of the location, clear across the city. Surprised by the unexpected announcement, she had naively asked what date they had set, thinking them a little young but also hoping there would be enough time to search out proper attire for the big event. This had drawn blank stares and uncomfortable silence.

Matthew had croaked something about things not having progressed that far while Heather sat there looking down into her empty coffee cup. It then seemed they had suddenly thought of somewhere else they had to be and had made a quick departure, leaving Lydia with no thought of urging them to extend their visit.

There had been a quick call placed to Lorraine which had only resulted in yet another unpleasant mother/daughter exchange. After that, she had stuck to her convictions and waited. And waited. Her daughter and her grandson both gone on with their lives.

"Well? What do you think?" Here was Matthew still waiting for an answer, arm still stretched out in a sweep of the room.

"Fine, very nice." What did he expect her to say? What would Malcolm say? She knew what he wouldn't say. He wouldn't say, this is not what we had envisioned for you. Do you have any idea how disappointed I am? She pictured her husband scowling at her, something he rarely did in life.

"Thank you for having me, Matt," she said softly. She reached over and took his hand, giving it a little squeeze. "You look happy, content."

Her grandson smiled at her. She had nearly forgotten that heart melting smile. "I am," he said. "And I hope you'll be happy with my announcement, the reason we've invited you and the others." He pulled his hand loose from her clasp and gave a shrill whistle through his teeth to get the attention of the other guests. Someone standing near the stereo lowered the volume, and the room grew quiet.

"Heather, get in here and join us," he called in the direction of the kitchen. The blond, permed Indian maiden appeared minus her headdress, swiping her hands dry on her jeans. Her gaze connected with Matthew's, a pleased conspiratorial look passing between them.

"Listen up, everyone," he began. "Heather and I felt like celebrating, and all of you are the ones we most wanted to share our plans with. Most of you know Heather has been working hard on her nursing degree, and she's graduated with honors."

"Way to go," someone shouted and applause broke out. A tall, lanky fellow standing nearest to her extended his arm in her direction, urging her to take his pulse. A girl in the corner pretended to faint into the arms of her companion, laughter all around. A slightly embarrassed Heather smiled, waving her arms to simmer them down.

"Okay, okay, my training tells me you all look the picture of health," she pronounced.

Matthew, enjoying the scene, waited patiently before going on. "So," he continued finally. "Now that my partner has met her goal - and I'm so proud of her, by the way - she has offered, no demanded, that she be allowed to turn the tables and keep this humble roof over our heads while I make something of myself."

Pausing here, he shot a sly glance toward his grandmother, her expression still tentative. "And bowing to pressure," he went on, feigning reluctance, "I'm headed back to school, hopefully for a degree in mechanical engineering. All signed up, classes start next month."

"Hey, hey! Go for it!" coming from across the room. Then a toast with raised beer cans. "To a great partnership. To a great couple."

Acknowledging the warmth and good wishes of their friends, Matthew said, "I just have to add, without Heather's faith in me I'd probably be moping along some slow road to nowhere for the rest of my life. Then again, maybe not, because," he turned to his grandmother, "I had some pretty special grandparents growing up. They influenced me more than they knew. I guess I just had to mature a bit to see that." He reached over and gave Lydia a bear hug. "I miss Gramps so much," he whispered.

Lydia felt herself clinging to his embrace, the room fading before her. She could find no words until finally she whispered, "I wish he could have been here."

Later she would wonder why she hadn't said all the other things in her heart. Probably because it wasn't necessary. Her grandson was rooted on solid ground after all. He needed no words of encouragement or advice from her. He had Heather for that. All he needed from her was love, her unconditional love. That, she could supply.

Now what she needed most was to go home, to sort things out, to have a talk with Malcolm. She needed to tell him that while he was teaching Matt to use a compass, he had been pointing him in all the right directions. But then she suspected Malcolm knew that all along.

~~~~~~~~~~~~

*A new friend is desperately
in need of help in...*

FELLOW

The hour was early, and Bentwood Park at the north end of the city was all but deserted. The joggers had headed home to shower and change; the groundskeepers were still sipping their first cups of coffee over at Peppy's Diner; and the elderly park bench shift wasn't due til mid-morning.

A heavy-set figure in sweatshirt and backpack entered the park from Columbus Avenue. Maneuvering with an awkward, uneven gait, he scuffed his way along a path lined with carefully tended beds of petunias and geraniums and headed directly for the nearest trash container.

There, he slipped off the backpack and placing it at his feet, leaned over to search through the uncollected trash. By the time he straightened up, he had three discarded soda cans cradled between his forearm and body. He placed each in turn to his lips, threw his head back and with a long sucking sound, drained whatever remained of the sweet, sticky contents. After each, he swiped at his mouth with the back of his hand then stooped and deposited his find in the backpack.

"Five cents and five cents is ten cents and five cents is fifteen cents," he muttered. When finished, he re-zipped the pack and lifted it into place.

He moved on. His next stop produced four more cans and the procedure was repeated without variation. Each five cents painstakingly added until he had accurately calculated his bonanza.

By the time he neared the playground area, he had tallied up a grand total of thirty-five cents before becoming distracted. He enjoyed the park and came often, but early morning was his favorite time. At this hour the playground was empty, and he had his choice of equipment, and... there were no mothers casting disapproving glances his way. No one to say why don't you get off and give the little children a turn. No one to say hey, you're going to break that!

He didn't like it when people were cross with him, but he couldn't help it if he liked to swing. Maryellen and Gary both said it was okay because the swings were good and strong, but it was Maryellen who said it would be a good idea to come nice and early since he liked being up early anyhow.

The idea of scouting for returnable soda cans came to him later, like a reward. He loved money almost as much as swinging, but he loved Maryellen and Gary best of all. They were his friends, and they looked after him and the other guys - Richie and Wally and Roger and Patrick. They were all just like real family.

He selected the end swing, which was set higher than the rest, and sat down. Grabbing the cold chains, he backed up until his toes were barely in contact with the ground, then pulled his feet up. He was off, head thrown back, gliding through the still morning air. He closed his eyes because it seemed to magnify the motion. It was a glorious sensation that calmed and soothed. Back and forth he floated.

Time was of little consequence. He could swing forever with his eyes shut, and he did just that until he heard voices close by. Opening his eyes, he saw a young boy tugging a woman in his direction.

"Over there," the sturdy little towhead pointed. "I wanna go over there and swing."

Territory established, the first arrival sat very still and waited for the woman's reaction. He was used to rejection and accepted it matter-of-factly. He was prepared to leave if necessary.

The woman's gaze was fixed directly on him, assessing. She permitted the youngster to pull her closer and finally, decision made, she relaxed her grip on his hand. The little one raced to the nearest swing and pulled himself up. Three empty seats separated the two.

They ignored one another, each engrossed in his own solitary pursuits. One challenged the apparatus, straining, demanding. The other doddled, stopping frequently to carve depressions in the soft dirt underfoot with the toe of his shoe.

After a time, curiosity tempted the young child to turn and stare directly at his swinging companion, whose placid face was still tilted skyward, eyes still shut. Silently, the lad slipped off his seat and took a new one next to the object of his interest.

"What's your name?" the child asked.

"Gordie," came the reply, eyes still shut.

"Gordie," the child repeated. "My name is Justin, and that's my mommy." He pointed toward the woman who had retreated some distance away and was now crouching by a petunia bed. She was faced away from them.

Gordie opened his eyes. "What's she doin?"

The child shrugged, unconcerned. He was more interested in his new acquaintance, and he peered intently into Gordie's face. The eyes were dark and wide-set; the sandy brown hair grew thick and low on his forehead.

"You have whiskers," Justin announced with the simple directness of the very young. "Are you a man or a boy?"

"I'm a fellow," Gordie replied without hesitation. "Gary says we're all fine fellows."

The child appeared satisfied, and the two fell silent. Only moments later, Justin chirped up again. "Know how much I am?"

Gordie shook his head.

"This many." To demonstrate, he slipped to the ground and held up a fat little hand, four fingers pointing straight up, his thumb tucked carefully away.

Gordie nodded. "I'm this many," he said, holding both hands out, fingers spread wide. Retracting them into fists, he thrust them forth again.

Justin looked bewildered. "That's a lot," he said simply.

"Look, your mother's digging up those flowers," Gordie blurted out, leaping to a brand new thought.

"She could get arrested!"

"Could not," the little boy shouted. He began to whimper at the thought.

Gordie had frightened the child. He knew he had. In conciliation, he stuck his hand into a pocket and produced a sourball wrapped in cellophane. He held it out.

His new friend accepted the offering, quickly unwrapping the candy and popping it into his mouth. He moved it into his left cheek giving his little face a lopsided chipmunk look.

Gordie felt better. New friends weren't easy to find. "Want to learn how to pump?" he asked. He demonstrated, pulling back with his arms while thrusting his legs straight out. He leaned way back, tilting his face skyward. "Try it," he commanded.

Justin did as he was told.

Lean back more when you go forward," his teacher instructed. He demonstrated once more.

The child watched closely and tried again, assuming a more flat-out position. "Is this good, Gordie?" He drew his breath in to say something further, but the sourball slid out of his cheek and into his throat.

Gordie watched him slip off the swing seat to the ground, landing on his hands and knees. The strange, throaty sounds coming from the child frightened him, and he did the only thing he could think to do. He slipped off his own swing and reached down to clap the little boy on the back. No result. He tapped again.

Justin continued to make strange sounds, and Gordie felt panic swell up and engulf him. It was all his fault, and he wanted to run away. Instead, he forced himself to holler, causing the child's mother to turn in their direction. At once, she was on her feet and running toward them, trowel discarded, hair flying.

Gordie didn't wait until she reached them. He turned away and ran toward the nearest exit and on to Linden Street. By the time he had covered the short distance, his pulse was pounding in his ears, his breath coming in short gasps.

He stepped off the sidewalk and leaned into the inside lane of traffic, wildly waving his arms. Please, Please, he mouthed. It was simultaneously a plea to the motorists and a prayer to the heavens.

Traffic was peaking. Cars of every description rushed past, their occupants insulated in little worlds of their own. No one paid attention to a pathetic figure frantically waving his arms from the gutter.

It was no use. Gordie wanted to cry, but he had a man's job to do. He must get help for his new little friend. He must! He looked back across the park. He could see the hunched figure of the mother but nothing more. Justin was still on the ground, out of sight.

Now frantic, Gordie took another step closer to the traffic, leaning further out. A blue Escort slowed, and the driver eyed the young fellow, made a quick judgment, accelerated, and was gone. Tears came now, and Gordie started to run once more along the sidewalk. He wished he had never left the house this morning. He wished he was up in his own room behind the closed door, safe from trouble and decisions that accompanied troubles.

Then, as if tapped by a magic wand, a desperate thought jumped out at him. It was something he shouldn't even consider, but as the idea came into focus, so too did the very thing he was now looking for. It was practically right in front of him. He hesitated only a brief moment. "Not supposed to," he said out loud. And then, "I gotta, I gotta."

It couldn't have been more than moments, but it seemed like hours as he wrapped his arms around the pole for comfort and waited, looking in both directions. He heard them before he saw anything. Sirens screaming. Two trucks bearing down on the very spot where he stood rooted.

The first man off the lead truck eyed Gordie suspiciously. "Did you pull that?" His manner was menacing and accusing. "Speak up," he commanded. "Where's the fire?"

Just when he needed it most, Gordie's voice failed him, the muscles in his throat knotting up. He couldn't speak so he did the next best thing; he pointed back up the street where now, in plain sight, the woman was stumbling toward them, the limp form of the boy in her arms. The terror on her face was plain even at that distance.

The men, seeing her then, ran. Gordie remained behind, no more able to move than he was to speak. He wrapped his arms even tighter around the pole.

When he dared allow himself a look, he saw only the backs of men kneeling on the ground. Then another siren and an ambulance rounded a distant corner and approached, squealing to a stop in front of the group. Gordie looked away. His whole body heaved with inaudible sobs. "Hate you, Gordie; hate you, Gordie." He murmured it over and over.

The next thing he was aware of was a firm hand on his shoulder. "Son, what's your name? Son?" It was one of the black-suited firemen.

"Gordie Bemis," came the weak reply. "I didn't mean to make him die...gave him candy to make him feel better...didn't mean to kill him...he was my friend." The words tumbled out and ran together. The anguish was so apparent and so acute; the man knew he must allow it to run its course. He waited.

When, at length, Gordie had exhausted himself, the man took his turn. "Son, everything is going to be all right. The little boy was revived; he'll be okay. He's going to the hospital to be checked over, that's all."

Gordie was confused. He had expected anger, but what he heard was kindness, much like when Gary talked things over with him. For the first time, he raised his head and looked directly into the man's face.

The firefighter had had sufficient time to assess Gordie and was visibly moved. On impulse, he threw his arms around the poor chap and embraced him. "Son," he said, "what you did to save your little friend was clear-headed and courageous. You're to be commended."

The message was slowly sinking in. No one was mad at him. Justin was okay. And he was - what did the man say - courageous. He had made a decision without asking Maryellen or Gary, and they were going to be proud of him.

"Do you live nearby?" The man's question brought him back abruptly. He nodded.

"Sorry we can't give you a lift; against the rules. But maybe you'd like to come down to the main station. The chief will be there tomorrow, and I know he'd like to meet you. Would you like that?"

Gordie was overcome. Would he like to? You bet! Again his voice failed him, and he could only nod.

The man reached for Gordie's hand and shook it firmly. "Good. We'll see you then. Don't forget now!" He smiled, turned, and rejoined his companions.

Gordie watched until his vision was totally obscured by other traffic. His head was spinning. There was so much to remember. He didn't want to leave out a single detail when he related his story. And then there were plans to make for tomorrow. He would ask to borrow Patrick's blue blazer...and Roger's red tie...and have his hair cut...and look for his good shoes...and, of course, ask everyone to go with him.

As he started along, the clanging of cans from the pack on his back reminded him of an important stop to make on the way home. He hoped Mr. Rooney at the corner store wasn't too busy today. Mr. Rooney always greeted him the same way. "What's new with you, Gordie?" He wanted to tell his friend everything.

A chance meeting signals
the hint of a future together in...

over coffee

He was on in years; so was she. Is that, the newlyweds wondered, why people wanted to know how they met? Everyone they knew asked it. She thought it intrusive. He saw it simply as friends interested in friends. So they shared bits and pieces of their story. She reluctantly, he eagerly.

Two strangers selecting Christmas wreaths on a blustery December day. Both eyeing the same large dellarobia creation. Each reaching out, gloved hand touching gloved hand. He deferring to her. She changing her mind, unsure. He returning to the original selection. Decisive.

Neither recalls who started the casual exchange that followed, but they agree it had begun with a remark about times present versus times past. They are both front-door people it seems, shaking their heads at those aware only of the garage door at the end of the drive. That flat, plain expanse dutifully swinging up at the push of a button.

They stand there forgetting the deep chill of the day, remarking about the many houses with driveways scraped clean but no path shoveled to the front door. The charming, inviting door with character, ignored and forgotten. People within, they decide, are sending a clear message. Do not come calling.

They also aren't absolutely sure who suggested continuing the discussion at the bakery across the street. She is sure she would never have been so bold. He, raising his eyebrows in silent contradiction.

Over coffee - his black, hers light, no sugar -

they reminisce about the good old days when friends and family dropped in by invitation or simply whim. When the ring of the doorbell announced something more than a local candidate, flyer in hand, asking for support. The scout troupe soliciting canned goods. No, it had triggered the anticipation of cherished hours spent sharing food and lively conversation.

Each means to keep the tone impersonal, talking in generalities. Just ten or fifteen minutes out of two lives on a fading winter afternoon. But a certain comfort level quickly sets in, catching them by surprise, controlling the moment. Natural reserve thawing. Maybe it was the warmth or the aroma suggesting the intimacy of one's own kitchen. They signal for refills on their coffee and order two muffins. Hers lemon poppy, his carrot and raisin.

At some point he sheds his jacket, draping it over the back of his chair, revealing a leaner, more angular look hidden beneath the bulk of the outerwear. And she, loosening her coat, lets it fall away, exposing a figure plumped and softened by the passage of years. They survey one another, surreptitiously. None of the blatant ogling of the young. None of the critical assessment of middle age. A general acceptance of what was. Nature had exacted a toll, but she had not been unkind.

They speak then of losses and disappointments, of joys and triumphs, sharing guarded glimpses into their pasts. Completed careers. Spouses, gone but not forgotten. Children scattered, and grandchildren carrying on the family name if not the traditions.

*Coffee cups are drained, his muffin gone,
hers left half eaten. They take no notice of the time until
the waitress, approaching, deposits the single check
carefully between them. Two ungloved hands at once
reaching, touching, withdrawing. Repressed stirrings;
each feigning nonchalance. An agreement - she
insisting - to split the charge. Magic interrupted.*

*Two people, not quite strangers, emerging.
Coats replaced, bodies insulated against the late
afternoon cold. Only the psyche left unprotected. He
heads east; she turns west. Tomorrow, they say.
Tomorrow we'll meet and walk. Tomorrow we'll walk
and admire front doors. Inviting front doors. Neglected
front doors. All of them.*

And that, they said, as friends gathered round, was how
it all began. And the friends smiled and nodded and
wished them well.

~~~~~~~~~~~~~~~~

A CLEARER VIEW (Poem)

A CLEARER VIEW

My eyes have changed, maturing
  over the years
And now they are focused
  with single purpose
To illuminate and expand
  my field of vision
So that now...

I see the value in patience
  when things are slow to unfold
I see what begs attention
  and what squanders precious time
I see the logic of moderation
  in all things material
I see I need not strive to impress
  if you are a true friend
I see your point of view
  without the urge to challenge
I see what matters most in life
  and what I can do without
It took a lifetime
  To see from within
But at last I see
  I truly see.

Patricia Carroll-Smith

Dear Reader,

I hope you have enjoyed my stories. They have been labor of love, produced over time – a very long time – as evidenced in "Fellow" by the fact there were no cell phones and   no opportunity to dial 911 in that particular story.

"The Side of the Road" came into being following walks I have taken, stopping to smell the lilacs along the way. Who can resist when they burst into bloom!

Otto Carr, Edwina Steinway and Cora Davenport were floating around in my head for ages before I found a place for them in "A Trip for Morris."

Perhaps you found you could easily replace Fiona's name in "What's Good for the Goose…" with one from your experiences. Enough said about that!

As for "At the Mall," I love the cinnamon rolls at Cinnabon. What other excuse does one need for a story?

The rest simply developed a life of their own after many rewrites. Thank you for taking the time to read them whether during a coffee break as the title suggests, a long wait at the doctor's office, or simply an idle hour here and there.

Regards,

PCS

IN APPRECIATION

My heartfelt gratitude to Paula Freda for patiently guiding me through the steps needed to bring my stories into this format.

Also, a big thank you to my grandson, Jeffrey Rawson, who came to the rescue when the updated and improved? changes on my new computer refused to cooperate with my outdated mind.

Made in the USA
Charleston, SC
27 November 2016